Serpens Abyss
A Novella

T.D. Nutt

DEDICATION

For my loving and supportive wife, wonderful daughters, and caring family.

.

CONTENTS

ABOUT THE AUTHOR

T.D. Nutt is a creative writer, disabled veteran, and student. Mr. Nutt is currently working on his Bachelor of Fine Arts degree in Creative Writing for Entertainment. When he isn't writing, he's spending time with his wife, two daughters, and their two crazy dogs..

1 THE TRAIL OF NOAH THORNE

"This hearing is to determine if Noah Thorne is guilty of genocide and treason."

"Noah Thorne you may now state your defense."

I glance around the intergalactic criminal court at its gold facade then back to the five judges running the proceedings.

"I've been beaten, hung, and left for dead, and that was one of my good days. On my bad days, well, I was shot, blow up, and died so often I lost count. It all started after my twenty-seventh birth year celebration."

Twenty Months Ago

I was sent to investigate reports of child sacrifices and cannibalism on the planet of Sinity.

I witnessed the worst of humanity at its vilest and most sickening. Somewhere along the way, I made a mistake because I woke up bleeding and staked to the ground.

I was left out as a sacrifice to the giant red firestorm ants that lived inside the planet's soil. Soon, I experienced the touch of probes from their antenna.

I knew then their horrible bites would follow; I weighed the options of a new life versus one surrounded by constant violence and death.

The gold Galactic Marshal's badge pinned to my chest had slowly become a millstone. With each day, I no longer felt the pride that I once had at seeing it, only its immense weight on my shoulders.

The day was a perfect day to die. The yellow sky was clear with no signs of tornadoes on the horizon, a rare sight since the terraforming. I tried to focus the glare off my badge onto the ropes.

The ants grew bolder and their bites more frequent. I was sure I was going to die without ever having a chance to raise a family.

In my agony, I smelled burnt rope, and was able to get one hand free.

Three days later, I was back on the capital planet of Capula One. A smoky haze covered the city.

I felt alone as I walked into the Senate building and handed in my badge and guns. I meet with the former Chairwoman of Senate Oversight.

"Madam Chairwoman, I need a chance at a family, I'm sorry."

"Mr. Thorne, I understand and good luck."

I grabbed the nearest shuttle and flew straight to Julie, "I want to spend the rest of my life with you. Will you marry me?"

"Yes...yes, Noah."

"I quit the Marshal service today and purchased a small ranch on Cimarron Forty-Five."

"Really, Noah? You did that for me?"

"Yes; of course, you should see the ranch nestled in the snow tipped mountains.

The simple ranch house surrounded by clear blue lakes and tall wavy purple grass a perfect place to raise our family."

"Our family. I like the sound of that," she remarked.

"I want to get married immediately. Let's sell everything and leave as soon as possible."

"Noah! Right now?"

"Yes, let's do it leave everything in the past and go find new lives."

"Okay, yes."

We married that day, boarded a ship, and set out on our honeymoon voyage. The first few days passed without incident.

We let the AI set the course and indulged in other activities. On the fourth day, we encountered a meteor shower.

"Julie, we need to reroute."

"Noah, what does the nav-system say?"

"It plotted a new course, but it takes us out of protected space."

"Is it safe?"

"Julie, we have no choice. The meteors will tear through this ship's hull."

Our luck worsened when two days later a random ION storm hit our ship.

"Noah, the navigation array is damaged."

"Can the nav-system still plot or is it fried?"

"Noah, it's gone!"

"We need an inhabitable world."

"Noah, I saw one on the display it's not far from here."

"Can you remember the general direction?"

"Yes, I think so. Oh, Noah, I'm scared."

"We'll be all right and we're together."

Sixty hours later, we caught a glimpse of Purgatory Nine.

"Julie, this isn't good. This world is an outlaw paradise."

"Noah, what should we do?"

"We've crossed the point of no return." I said,

"We have to land or crash now."

We landed and were hit by the weight of the severe heat as soon as we left the ship.

But, we started walking across the dry; crimson desert surface.

"Noah? Why don't you like this place?"

"Not too long ago, an inter-dimensional wormhole opened in the Nebula. The Wormhole spat out the deadliest and vilest murderers, thieves, prostitutes, and swindlers. The violent horde descended and raided this world's most precious metals. They also made Purgatory Nine their new home."

"Oh Nova," Julie said, "Noah, what are we walking into?"

"No idea," I answered, "There are some good people here, but this planet is the most dangerous and unstable place in Serpens Abyss."

"Noah people are headed this way."

"Well hello, what are y'all doing out here?" the man with the pockmarked face asked.

"Our ship lost its navigation array, and we

were forced down," I answered.

"In that case, we would be happy to help," the pockmarked man said.

"We need to buy a used array," I stated.

"Going to cost you," the pockmarked man replied.

"We've only got four hundred Kravens," I said, "I hope it will be enough to buy a used array."

A slender man toward the back of the group pipes in, "Sorry, mister but we deal only in gold around here."

"Is there an exchange?" I asked, "I could convert the Kravens to gold."

"Enough of this crap," a hawkish faced man said, "Give us your gold or die."

"We don't have any gold," Julie said, "Noah just told you that."

"You shut your mouth, woman," the pockmarked man said to Julie.

"Cut the attitude," I told him, "that's my wife."

"Tough guy, huh," a chubby man said as he

drew a laser pistol.

Someone told these men we had gold, nudged them in our direction, and let them loose. The twelve of them proceeded to beat me and then they took us to a derelict mining town.

The men started raining blow after blow down upon me and asked for gold again; I kept telling them that we didn't have any gold.

But, they wouldn't listen. After a few hours, they stopped punching and kicking me.

The pockmarked man gave me a tobacco stained grin as he took out a rope and dangled it in my face.

2 THE DEATH OF JULIE REDFORD

The men were drunk, angry, and stupid, three things that should never mix. After beating Noah for hours, they wobbled about on unsteady feet.

Unable to continue and covered in his blood they lay around the fire and drank some more.

Julie was forced to witness everything they did to Noah. Cold terror gripped her mind, and it snapped unable to comprehend their sadistic actions.

In her agony and despair, she found her voice. She began to scream as they placed her husband onto a nearby box, a rope around his neck.

The pockmarked man with black teeth smiled

at her and kicked the box away. The men turned and mocked her grief.

Julie lifted her head up and watched as dark passions grew behind their eyes.

"We going to take her back for the money?" the hawkish-faced man asked.

"I want to see what's so special about her," the pockmarked man said.

Unable to stop them as they lunged forward ripping at her clothing. She fought.

Her nakedness revealed to all; there were too many. Fist and boots descended upon Julie, beating her into unconsciousness.

The last moments of her young life slowly passed away with a futile whimper and one last gasp.

.

3 THE HANGING OF NOAH THORNE

The box flew out from under me, and I had the perception of floating. Then, I was falling. A sudden jerk of the rope, then intense pain, and overwhelming darkness settles.

Unconsciousness claimed me, and I waited for the white light. It didn't come, and I awakened to silence. I tried to open my eyes, but my neck was sending nonstop pain signals to my brain.

The hairs on my arms rose as I felt a cold desert night breeze. The powerful wind moved me into the ebb and flow of a swinging motion. My inner ear detected a small creaking noise that soon erupted into a sharp snap.

Then I experienced the familiar sensation of falling once again. When able to stand, I glanced at the hanging tree. The fools tied the rope to a rotten limb. I shuffled over to a bloody lump on the ground.

Julie's naked and beaten, unrecognizable as human just a bloody mess of flesh. I had to shoo away hungry rats that had swarmed all over her body.

Inside an ember of rage began to flame into a burning pit of madness as I gaped at her raped and murdered corpse my eyes grew hot with hatred. I used the hate to fuel me as I dug into the frozen red ground with my hands.

Once I buried Julie, I stood my heart black with vengeance as I stumbled and crawled to the nearest spaceport. Stole a ship, removed the Ident, and set a course back to my badge and guns.

As the ship left Serpens Abyss, I crawled inside the medical regeneration chamber. I woke up some time later in a different constellation.

The chamber regenerated several broken bones and patched broken ribs. It was unable to repair the rope scar around my neck. I saw the scar as a symbol of my bitter blackened soul now twisted and burned by hate.

It also said I had died for two minutes. I eventually made it back to Capula One. On the capital planet of the Galactic Alliance, I asked for a meeting with the Senate Chairwoman. I volunteered for what would either be a suicide mission or vengeance.

"Madam Chairwoman, I can clean up Serpens Abyss, but I need carte blanche."

"Mr. Thorn, we've wanted that system tamed for a while, but I need one more thing,"

"What?"

"This is off the books and personal. I need you to rescue my granddaughter. She was on Carus for a data collection mission. Last we heard she was caught and in the hands a dangerous man. Bring her home," the Chairwoman said.

"That all?"

"Yes, Marshal Thorne," she replied forgetting to mention that the man was an Empyrean Assassin.

"Stupid, Thorne, very stupid. Rule one you never volunteer. It always leads to trouble," I remark aloud berating myself.

As I attempt to guide the ship past, the Empyrean Navy patrols. The Class Seven Tridan is a small two-person scout ship. What the ship lacks in armor and firepower it makes up for in speed and stealth. Only one problem the Tridan has a huge wake field. Cloaked as I passed the patrols but if off on my calculations by a nanometer then they would have felt my wake and start hunting.

I was lucky to land on the Empyrean home world of Carus unscathed. After, hiding the ship I somehow got lost a couple of times on the dark lava planet. I made it to where the woman was being held captive.

I set up surveillance and studied the guard's patterns and timing. Once I had a clear picture of the place, I made my way inside. I found the young woman chained to a post in his bedroom.

She was hurt and bleeding. He had forced her to do sick and perverse acts. After I had used a mobile regeneration kit on her, she was able to move. We made it out of the building unseen.

Our luck disappeared as we approached the space dock. Carus Internal Security was everywhere, and they torture and kill for fun. They had found the ship we were trapped.

"Sorry that was our ride," I told the woman.

"There is another way," the woman said.

"Really?"

"He liked to talk. One time he bragged about a prototype they're testing," the woman said, "He called it their greatest gunship."

"Do you know where the testing area is located?" I asked.

She smiled despite her pain and replied, "Yep."

We stuck to the shadows of the lava-covered world and found the testing area. We had to walk down inside the blackened banks of a scorching lava river.

Our breathing became obstructed from the constant inhalation of ash. The brightness of it all was blinding, but we made it inside the area's perimeter.

Exhausted and sweating almost dehydrated I knew we only had one shot at stealing the ship. The gunship was a gorgeous, sleek red, and black Empyrean Navy Special Ops class. I could tell it had significant weapons and electronic upgrades.

"We need to make a run for the ship," I said to the woman, "Can you make it?"

"Yes."

I stared into her copper brown eyes and saw a fierce determination. I handed her my secondary weapon and told her to get ready.

"On the count of two. One. Two."

We began running across the launch platform. We made it halfway across before someone called out to us in surprise.

"Stop! Who are you?" an Empyrean guard yelled.

"Sound the alarm! Intruders!" shouted another.

We fired our yellow energy bolts slicing the air as we ran closer to the ship. Stenciled on the side was its designation *The Reaper*. We made it inside the docking bay, closed the hatches started launch procedures and took off. I quickly searched for the Ident, removed it, and started a hack.

4 THE TAMING OF SERPENS ABYSS

One Stellar Year Later

The Reaper glided stealthily through Serpens Abyss a demilitarized nebula. The abyss is also, an essential part of contested space. The dark, lava worlds of the war addicted Empyrean Constellation on one side, constantly plotting universal domination.

On another, the arid, sand worlds of the Haijarin Death Cultist. The rest of the surrounding systems were all part of the Galactic Alliance. All three governments were salivating over Serpens Abyss and its strategic uses and minerals.

All three factions using proxies in a never-ending shadow war. None considered a safe or healthy choice by any of the independent-minded people of the abyss.

Inside *The Reaper's* metal hull, I lay awake, staring at the gunmetal gray ceiling over my berth. I couldn't shut off the memories of that fateful day. The day they turned me into a hunter of men.

The actions that made me into a crestfallen man who understands weapons better than people. I rolled over and pondered the brown bottle on a nearby bookshelf. I told myself. Its comfort is only a mirage. The temptation was too strong; it pulled me into its liquid depths.

After a few too many swigs, I set the bottle down. My bones and joints voiced their defiance as I climbed out of my bunk. The popping echoed in the metal room, reminding me of that same beating.

I tried to remember the faces of the men, but all I could pull from the haze were voices.

"Holo-display on, show all wanted posters," I ordered the ship's computer.

I studied every face for the thousandth time. In the end, I waved the display away in frustration none of them were familiar.

"Holo-display off."

Still, the intoxicating aroma of freshly brewed coffee brightened my day. I followed the smell into the galley and poured a large cup. I gazed out of the large bay window as I took a sip. The sweetness before the acidity hit my throat, comforted me.

A small red planet was orbiting below, taunting me. Purgatory Nine, a reddish hell taken straight from the depths of my nightmares and sitting there as a constant reminder of my greatest heartbreak.

Almost ten stellar years the planet has been without a planetary justice system, one since Julie's death. I'm the man who volunteered to tame this world and bring justice to the abyss.

I witnessed the first of its two red suns rise behind the planet's mountains. Then beheld as Purgatory Nine's dry surface, was bathed red by the sun's crimson light.

Cursed myself for the distraction because I didn't see Rose enter or stand beside me.

"Noah, you okay?" She inquired.

Rose Harper is the only person since Julie to call me Noah, and I don't know why it feels right.

"Sorry, Rose lost in thought."

When I first inventoried the ship, I found a synthetic humanoid. After a few modifications, I designated it Sam. I had Sam go down to scout. I'm waiting for his report. My sub-dermal implant beeped. Sam found a target.

"Rose, the ship is yours."

"Be safe, Noah."

"Welcome back to Hell," I groaned as lifeless cherry colored dust and desert rushed towards the landing craft.

The lander touched down outside Tuarala, home to Purgatory Nine's finest criminals. The word town would be a loose definition of it, more like a horrible dust-covered wooden place with more graves on Boot Hill than buildings. Built only for functionality, not comfort.

"Boss, the mosquito drone is active, and you should overhear his voice now," Sam remarked.

"Negative on voice he's not one of our guys. Capture DNA profile," I replied.

The badge on my chest was gaining a lot of attention as I walked down Saloon Street. The grimy street was beginning to fill, and I sensed trouble on the wind. An unseemly warm wind blowing through the streets like an angry child as it tossed and threw everything about.

"Well, law dog you lost or just stupid?" Jackson bellowed as he swatted a mosquito off his dark brown skin. "Doesn't matter because you're about to die, and I'm going to take that badge as a trophy."

I gave the enormous man one of my rare smiles. I scanned his face, and the drone's DNA data displayed on my internal visual interface.

Bill Jackson, warrant active, sentence death. About time, I established my place in the pecking order and checked off a warrant.

"I'm Marshal Noah Thorne, and you've got a death warrant," I announced, as my visual interface turned off.

Jackson smiled and glanced at the crowd for support and laughter. He removed his shirt and flexed for the crowd.

Ignoring Jackson's grandstanding; I punched him in the throat, damaging his windpipe. Then, I shoved my palm under his jaw with all my might. His head jerked back, spraying blood and tongue from his mouth.

I finished Jackson off with a right cross to the side of his face. The blow broke open old scar tissue, peeling back skin, and the whiteness of bone showed through. No movement or sound from the crowd. The bystanders were stunned by the brutality and quickness of the fight. They witnessed in awe as the mighty bully Bill Jackson bleed out on the red dusty street.

5 THE CHANGES OF PERCEPTION

I was soaking my bruised right hand as I sat at my desk and relaxed in the Ready Room.

Rose timidly entered and for the first time, I noticed her silken skin, shapely figure, and pouting lips.

My breath caught. Rose was a crewmate, but now I saw her as a woman. I rubbed the back of my neck and pushed the thought away. A bizarre expression crossed her face.

Trouble?

"W-word is the Empyrean Grand Inquisitor put a bounty on your head for a million Kravens," Rose reported.

"Wow, for that much I'd shoot myself. Guess, I better lock up your weapons also," I joked.

"No, I would do it for free," she teased.

Our eyes locked, and tension rose in the air. An unspoken change in us took place. Rose's eyes were almost glistening. She was crying. I must've crossed a line somewhere.

Did I upset her? I cut the thought short and joked, "I'll watch my back." As I tried to ease the tension.

"All joking aside, it seems Julie's father still blames you for her death," Rose remarked changing the subject.

Thank you. I thought, but instead, I went with, "Looks like it."

Hell, I blamed me I knew we should have gone elsewhere. Every night I re-experienced the beating until my scars burned with an awakening pain. My bed and clothes would be damp from that night's sweat.

I stood up, gazed in the mirror, and traced the rope scar on my neck.

6 THE DESIRES OF ROSE HARPER

Noah is in there bruised, and I can't comfort him; Nova I hate this. Nova, give me the strength to go in there and tell him that I'm in love with him.

Rose pushed the thought aside and entered the room there was Noah sitting behind his desk. Six feet of broken man in need of a gentle touch.

I want to reach out, run my fingers through his wavy black hair. Trace my finger down his strong jaw and dimpled chin. Pull him close and whisper everything will be all right. I can't do this. I can't screw up our friendship.

Rose was lost in her thoughts as she stood in the room. She soon realized Noah was gazing at her with a bizarre expression.

Rose, you need a reason to be in here. Think. Tell Noah, about the bounty, stupid.

She thought fast and reported the latest news to Noah. He smiled, told a joke, and she was off the hook.

I love his sense of humor.

She thought as she teased him back.

Was that too flirty?

Her panicked thoughts were muddled as they locked eyes.

Oh, Nova his eyes. His blue eyes are like staring into a chasm while a storm rages within intense, dangerous, and glorious.

She was caught by her thoughts and carried away as the mood changed. She could recognize the penetrating attraction for the first time.

I've wanted this for so long. No, he has an expression of concern on his rugged face.

Her eyes were glistening as months of fear and tension leave her body.

These are tears of joy, you big, stubborn fool of a man.

Noah makes a bad joke.

He's trying to cheer me up not succeeding but trying.

Rose shoved her depressing thoughts aside and let him off the hook.

7 THE WARRANTS OF THE ABYSS

I turned from the mirror back to Rose, forced myself to get back on track.

"Whose next on our warrant list?" I asked.

"Leon Manning," She responded, "A friend of yours from the old days, I believe."

"He's no friend of mine. That sorry maggot left ten of us to die on Solas during a gunfight," I answered through gritted teeth. "Given the chance, I'll put him down faster than a snake bite."

"Sorry," Rose replied.

"Not your fault, you didn't know. The mission was off the books," I answered shrugging.

"Good news is he's running an outlaw gang

east of here," Julie continued.

"Why is this system so important to the Senate?" I asked suddenly.

"Think of the benefits of a galactic space hub here next to an inter-dimensional wormhole," Rose replied. "One that belongs to a genuinely independent system."

"Beholden to no one? No Corporations, the Empyreans, or the Haijarians?" I asked.

"Yes."

I shook my head at her naiveté.

"Never happen," I told her. "No way the Empyrean Legion will sit by and let it happen."

She seemed confused by my attitude. I understood. She was an idealist. I was a realist.

"They need every ounce of gold and silver off this rock to fund their perpetual war machines," I explained. "Just to put things in perspective, I'm Kill on Sight by the Empyrean Legion and any lowlife bounty hunter with a gun. So shoot me stop the changes."

She nodded.

"Where the Empyrean Legion goes death follows," I continued. "As you know anywhere death happens on a massive scale the death worshiping Haijarian cult won't be far behind."

She nodded again, and I could see the gears moving in her head. Rose was my Intelligence Officer, and also my liaison with the Senate. I needed her to understand what we are up against out there.

"Oh, and yours truly is also Kill on Sight by all Haijarian cult members. For supposedly insulting their religion when I executed Guru Rumal."

"No one told me you were the one that shot Rumal," Rose replied.

"All a smokescreen to fool the low-level members. I was able to make the Guru talk before the end. He provided names of everyone within the top circle of the cult," I explained as I shook my head. "I broke past their vow of silence, and they know fear for the first time, so they need me gone."

She was starting to make the connections.

I rubbed my wolf hybrid's belly as I waited. Dogg is my best friend and constant companion. The locals in Serpens Abyss were a superstitious lot. They believed black dogs are portents of death. They even killed them in birth. I rescued this Wolf/Dog hybrid from a similar fate.

"I'll check if the Senate will throw in some special gear. Maybe I can pick up some rations for Dogg. The poor thing needs red meat he is part wolf after all," she suggested.

"He can hunt for himself, not my fault the dummy won't go more than fifty steps from my side," I replied.

"Don't pretend you don't like the attention," Rose answered with a laugh.

She departed for Capula One in her shuttle, and for some reason I was lonely.

8 THE DANCE OF TUALARA

I knew the history by heart, but the fine citizens of Purgatory Nine wanted to show us how civilized they were. They put together a dance. Even went so far and selected two local students to give presentations on the history of the galaxy.

I rubbed the black stubble on my face and chin, a sign that I'm frustrated. Most people recognized the signal and gave me a wide berth. Regrettably, the back slapping Mayor didn't.

"Marshal Thorne, You will be so impressed by these young kids. Yes, sir!"

"I'm sure I will Mayor."

"They are two of our best and brightest, and I'm not just saying that because one of them is my son."

"You've done your town proud with this little ten-hour long event," I replied.

He missed the sarcasm. "Ah, here is the first one," the Mayor stated steering me towards the stage.

A small, scared girl named Janet Simmons took the stage, and with a trembling voice started.

"First, the emptiness of space opened, and the first humans crossed into the unknown. On five ships called 'The Arks,'" she intoned. "The last gasp of a dying dimension. Filled to the brim with plant, animal, and human life they spread out among the stars. They colonized several inhabitable worlds in many different solar systems. Over time governments rose and fought battles. Generations were born and died. However, their descendants still felt a need to explore further into space. They are always seeking more worlds to conquer and greater riches to acquire."

"Thank you, fascinating," I told her. She smiled for the first time. "Wonderful how your schoolhouse produced such an excellent student."

The Mayor continued to the next student, his son.

"Next up, is Peter Jenson."

I glanced at Sam and stifled a laugh. The synthetic humanoid sprained an eyeball when he tried to roll his eyes.

"Centuries later in the Centaurs Galaxy on a caustic and forbidding world. One Empyrean warlord set out to make all nearby planets fall under his rule," Jenson maintained. "He accomplished his goal. For a time the people thrived, and technology advanced in the systems. Life was good on the central planets but unforgiving on the outer planets. Taxes and tariffs made farming and mining barely livable trades. As many older people here remember, grumbles became discontent and resentment turned into rebellion. The outer planets rose up and formed The Galactic Alliance. Soon, they declared war on the Empyrean people. Some of you are survivors so; I won't bore you with the details. The Galactic War lasted ten stellar years and raged across the systems. Empyreans began to live and breathe warfare. Their technology and Talon assassins almost won in the end. But after a significant Empyrean defeat at the Battle of Sunset Colony, an armistice was signed declaring a ceasefire. Unfortunately, ten years later we still have no peace treaty only an addiction to warfare."

"Thank you, Peter, well done," I said then gave my goodbyes. Turned towards the Mayor and added, "I need to leave now, and go do my nightly rounds."

9 THE GUNFIGHT IN BIG KATE'S SALOON

I finally made it outside after I shook hands with most of the town. I noticed the Mayor left in a hurry when someone whispered in his ear. He was headed in the direction of Saloon Street, I wondered why.

A sensation of electricity and fear was drifting on the air. Thunder rolled, and lightning flashed across the night sky. The storm worsened as I approached Big Kate's Saloon. The place was buzzing as I push open the heavy swinging doors and stepped inside.

Chaos surrounded the oak bar as a mob filled the main floor.

"We don't need a Marshal here!" an owlish shaped man declared.

"Yeah, life was good before he came," another man remarked.

"Good for those of you on the outside of the law," the Mayor articulated pushing his way through. "But for those that want a place to raise families, it was a living hell."

"Someone is getting bold, hate for something to happen to your family, Mayor," a rat-faced man replied.

"If something does happen to this gentleman's family. I will take it as a personal insult," I responded fingers tapping my gun handle.

The room went silent as every head turned in my direction. They were just three more outlaws looking for a fight. They stepped forward towards the center as people backed away.

I stood tall and welcomed the challenge. The outlaw had three laser pistols two feet away. A reflection from the mirror behind the bar caught my eye.

Another man on my back left held a sawed-off laser rifle.

I turned on my data display and scanned men before me. Jack Simmons, warrant not active, listed as an escapee from the prison planet Samarian Six. James Blake, warrant not active, also listed as an escapee. The rat-faced man was Tom Jenkins, warrant active, sentenced to death.

The fourth man was an unknown. He could have been backing my play or just waiting to shoot me in the back during the confusion. Odds, I'm not willing to gamble on with my life.

"Simmons and Blake, neither of you, have active warrants, so choose carefully," I announced. "Simmons think of your little girl. I enjoyed her speech. Don't you want to live long enough to do the same?"

"What about me?" Jenkins interjected his tone was mocking and defiant.

"Jenkins, your warrant is active," I replied, "Draw, or run, I shoot on the count of two. One."

Jenkins, true to his nature, went for his gun early as Simmons and Blake backed his play. I drew as I stepped forward into the incoming fire. My first yellow bolt burned a hole through Simmons' chest the smell of charred flesh, and cloth filled the air. I grabbed Blake by his sweaty cotton shirt and swung him towards Jenkins. His orange bolt scorched the insides of Blake's head.

Dropping my human shield, I fired a blistering yellow bolt into Jenkins. Swivel around and dove to my left as the fourth man fired his rifle. Its blue bolt burned a nasty groove across my thigh. I shot as I was in the air my aim hit high, oxidized the man's throat. Breathing hard, I holstered my blaster and used my retinal scanner on what was left of the man's face.

Nothing. No, data returned. Usually, it meant a data purge from the central database.

Only hired assassins did that. My third day on this red rock and I already need to call Senate Oversight about a dead Empyrean Assassin. As the first of many gray drops of rain fell upon the town.

10 THE AMBUSH OF BOX CANYON

After the shootout, people were more willing to talk and provided information. Sam received a tip that Manning's gang was operating nearby.

We had been going for days without rest in the blistering heat, and Sam hadn't complained once. Not sure if he were programmed to complain or if he knew better. As we flew the fly-bikes, crimson dust and grime landed on our bodies. The wind hardened it into an impenetrable clay shell in seconds. For the next two hours, the pace was stop and go. We eventually broke free from the cumbersome annoyance went half a mile and repeated.

"The hideout should be two miles up in the next box canyon," Sam remarked.

"How many did your man say to expect?"

"He thinks at least two members of Manning's gang are all that's there."

"We'll send in the 'sketter and use the DNA rounds to be safe."

We hunkered on top of the ridge and surveyed the canyon below. A single cabin with no guard and two fly-bikes are out front. Something was off.

"Sam I got a bad feeling," I stated, "This smells like a trap."

Sam pulled the tiny mosquito drone from his bag and sent it flying.

"Boss, 'sketter is away."

He closed his eyes and patched into the drone's feed. Sam flew it down the sharp cliff face over a tiny creek and into the open window.

"We've got a problem, Boss. There's more than two inside."

"Run scan."

Sam read off the details from his scan.

"Warrants are active on the other four. The Billings' brothers, and one more, Boss."

"Any Ident on the fourth guy?"

"One sec, Leon Manning, Boss."

"Six we can handle. We'll proceed as planned. Get DNA from the oldest Billings and Manning."

"DNA amassed, Boss."

"Ok, you sync your first shot with Billings I'll take Manning. The others are fair game."

I prepared for the shot by closing my eyes and enjoyed the brisk wind as it blew across the desert. I slapped in a fresh prototype DNA synchronized energy pack. The red bolts would lock on and track that target only. I looked through the optical sensors and picked a point of interest on the outside wall. Clicked to enhance and my target's head appeared. I took three deep breaths. When I let all the air out on the third one and sensed that beautiful little pause, I squeezed the trigger. My target's head exploded.

The inside of the cabin was chaos as Billings' head did the same. I acquired a new target and sent my next bolt. Sam dropped another. I swung and sent another energy bolt into a fleeing outlaw. The last outlaw was making a run on a fly-bike. I readjusted to lead him and sent an energy bolt in his direction. He fell off face first into the pinkish dust.

11 THE BLACKOUT OF TUALARA

The flight back to Tualara on our fly-bikes was as miserable as the flight out. We flew in during the middle of the dark time. The only light on the empty street was artificial. For the next six hours between one Sun setting and the other rising, this was the most dangerous time on Purgatory Nine.

"We've got company at two o'clock, Boss."

"You can see him?" I asked.

"Infra-red spectrum selection for my eyes," Sam replied.

"Nice," I answered, "What's he doing?"

"Waiting for a signal," Sam replied, "Ah, two more at ten and three."

"You wouldn't happen to network with the generators would you?" I inquired.

"Yep. Just say when Boss."

With no hesitation, "They're all yours. Do it."

The lights across the town winked out and plunged everything into complete darkness. The street flashed yellow with three bolts from Sam's ION blaster.

As the lights came back on, three strangers lay dead on the street. Retinal scans came back as Janus Security Officers, but one of the men wore a small Arrowhead tattoo. They were bounty hunters sent by the biggest corporation in the galaxy: The Arrowhead Syndicate.

At the same time, we overheard a growl, a scream, and what sounded like teeth biting into flesh. At the end of the far alley, we found a fourth man with his throat torn out. Over his mangled body was a giant black wolf with a bloodstained muzzle.

"I guess you can hunt," I told him, "Good boy, Dogg."

Dogg licked the blood off his muzzle and gave a soft, affectionate yip.

"Sniper had the drop on us for sure," Sam stated as he looked down the alley.

I picked up a dark piece of cloth. Its fabric changed colors with my touch. "Sniper was wearing an expensive masking cloak to hide from your scans," I replied.

"Smart, but he didn't count on a wolf's nose," Sam added while giving Dogg an affectionate pat.

12 THE DESTRUCTION OF SAHALA

Not long after, we received another tip. This time, three of the people responsible for Julie's death were on the Haijarian planet Sahala. We navigated our fly-bikes deeper into the barren desert. Stalked our prey, and encroached on the serenity of the dead. Mahakali was a hole in wall town surrounded by giant polished tombstones that rose out of the ground. Sinister monuments of their death worship. Perfect place to harbor the type of men we sought.

"Sam, what have you discovered about the Haijarians?"

"Just the little bit in the central database."

"Well, Sam, the Haijarians are a newer religion founded out here about hundred stellar years ago by a bandit. He was hiding in a cave from his men. A month later, he emerged with a new religion as protection. Made himself Jamaadaar and laid out the new dogma for his followers. He had taken and twisted parts of the Novarian Doctrine. Added child brides, slavery, world domination, and death worship into the mix," I explained.

"They fell for this?" Sam inquired.

"They accepted it because it gave them license to rape, kill, steal, and follow any perverse desire they wanted. After the first Jamaadar's death, the next one had a vision. He emerged the next day and added a new requirement for all followers." I paused and drew in a deep breath. "Planetary destruction as sacrifices to death and they had to give the inhabitants a choice to convert or die."

Sam glanced around at the sandy, desolate world and declared, "Not much of a choice."

We circled Mahakali in stealth mode and studied the layout everything covered under granules of sand. The Haijarians are gathering supplies preparing to leave. The underground water reservoirs are rumored to be running dry.

Mahakali was nothing more than a small settlement made long ago. By those who rejected a nomadic life and started building houses. The buildings were small stone multi-color constructions. Every one of them consisted of a central inner courtyard with rooms, and small walls surrounding the outside. Somewhere in this place sat my prey as they basked in their evil deeds.

"Boss, we got a hit in Quadrant 28-43," Sam stated as he surveyed the drone data.

"I only see sand and empty houses. Must be underground," I interjected.

"We have anything capable of opening a hole?" I asked.

"The prototype Particle-beam weapon on *The Reaper* can alter the atomic structure of the area."

"Fire for broad area effect," I ordered.

"Sam, can we do anything to jam their electronics?"

"Boss, the weapon should take care of that also. Once it hits, it will create radiation and send x-rays into the area that will disable any nearby electronics."

"Let's find out how good of a job the Senate Science Sanctum did. Fire," I ordered.

The Reaper hummed, and space lit up with a pulse of green as it sped towards us. Nothing could withstand the impact of mass traveling at light speed, and the explosion proved the rule. The ground shuddered and began to open. Secondary explosions started going off all around us. The ground fell and began to swallow everything around.

"Go!" I yelled, pulled Sam after me toward the fly-bikes.

We took off. The ground was falling away, and behind I could sense my fly-bike being pulled down with it. I dove for the rocks as the fly-bike fell into the sinkhole. Sam's synthetic hands took hold of mine, pulled me up onto the rocks to safety.

The world behind was gone. All we could see for miles was a giant hole.

"Did we do that?" I asked.

"Not sure, Boss."

"We need to make sure and fast. Run a full forensic scan pronto."

I prepared my report to send to the Galactic Senate along with my resignation when Sam called me over.

"You called it, Boss."

"What?"

"Every secondary explosion was an underground bunker. Each filled with Dreadnaught assault ships rigged for suicide flights," Sam explained.

"How many you reckon?"

"Total so far over a hundred thousand ships and data recovered from three of them show Capula One, Carus, and Solas as targets."

"Package your findings within this report and transmit all data to Senate Oversight."

Sam hesitated and inquired, "Umm, Boss you still want to send your resignation letter?"

"Yes."

He closed his eyes and linked up with *The Reaper*.

"Data packet sent," Sam declared, "Where to now?"

"Carus."

13 THE POLITICS OF JUSTICE

"Madam Chairwoman, I would like to raise a point if I may?" Senator Simon a small, round, and balding man interjected. He was known for his temper, and his ability to be bought.

"You may."

"This seems like a perfect opportunity to rid ourselves of a bad element."

"Bad element?" The Chairwoman challenged.

Madam Chairwoman was a distinguished figure in the Senate. She was known for her iron will and strong moral fiber. Worry was written on her typically happy face as of late. She hated to admit that as the oldest

Senator she now had the back pains of her age. It seemed the other Senators got younger, greedier, and dishonest with each election.

"Yes, these gunslingers wearing a badge, are nothing more than assassins," Senator Simon proclaimed.

"Senator Simon, your home world of Janus is under the control of a corporation, correct?" the Chairwoman challenged.

"Yes, we are protected by the Arrowhead Syndicate and are delighted with the arrangement."

"The Arrowhead Syndicate. Didn't they send four gunslingers to kill a Senate appointed Galactic Marshal?" she questioned.

"I don't know anything about that."

"Of course not, just a coincidence that it's the same, Marshal. Noah Thorne, the one they want for the substantial and illegal bounty. Happens to be the same one you are discussing today."

"I'm offended by that accusation," Senator Simon pronounced and raised his hands up in defense.

The Chairwoman waved him away, dismissing any further discussion. "Then let's drop the matter. Now if there are no other pressing matters I shall consider this discussion closed and reject the resignation of Marshal Thorne."

"Madam Chairwoman. What about Sahala?" Senator Simon demanded.

"I do sense the need to do something about that, and will be nominating both men for Valor medals. Good day, the meeting is adjourned," she declared.

14 THE SPACE BATTLE OF ANNE

I lay in my bunk and tried not think about Rose. Nope, I was not thinking about her long ebony hair as it caressed her tanned skin, her soothing voice, or her nymph like ears at all. I was solely focused on the job ahead. When my vidscreen beeped, Rose was all smiles on the other end, and it lifted my spirits.

"What put you in such a great mood?" I asked.

"Noah, I just spoke with the Senate Chairwoman. She rejected your resignation."

I nodded, hiding my relief. "How is your grandmother?"

"She's happy to see the day the Haijarians were wiped from existence," Rose replied.

"Harsh."

"She lost her birth planet to one of their attacks," she replied, tucking a strand of her raven black hair behind her ear.

"Oh, I never knew," I remarked.

"She doesn't talk about it, it was when my parents died, and she took me in."

"Sorry."

"Noah, she wanted me to tell you she owes you another favor."

"She doesn't owe me anything," I declared.

Rose sighed. "She thinks she does, and I'm not going to argue with her. She still thinks she owes you for helping me escape from Carus."

"We fled together," I answered correcting her.

"I remember. Just like hearing you admit once in a while you need help," Rose remarked getting the last jab at my ego before she disconnected.

A concerned Sam paged me to the bridge.

"Boss, we've got incoming ships closing fast."

"On my way."

I arrived, and there were several blips on the screen.

"Ident?" I asked.

"Empyrean Navy gunships, Boss."

"Must've been working on tracking our stealth drive," I added.

"Run or fight?" Sam requested.

"Prepare ship-to-ship weapons and let's introduce them to Anne," I ordered.

"Oh, they will love Anne," Sam stated with a nasty smile.

Anne is what we called our brand-new tactical AI. We found her on a crashed ship in the desert back on Purgatory Nine. The ship became trapped inside an inter-dimensional wormhole in some other existence. It ended up at the end of the wormhole above Purgatory Nine. All systems were damaged during the transfer, and it shattered upon impact. Anne was the only viable technology we recovered.

She could jam comm links between enemy ships, and was blindingly fast when calculating the best options for attacking and defense.

Anne could also coordinate the ion cannon network with the anti-ship missile launchers during space battles. All while simultaneously designing new defense grid systems.

"Hello, Sam and Noah," Anne announced as she began integrating with the ship's systems, "How can I assist you?"

"Darling, we are about to be attacked," I stated.

"No one's ever called me darling before," Anne declared, "I will protect you."

"See Sam. You need to understand how to talk to the lady."

Sam pointed past the window outside to a group of familiar objects. "Boss, this is contested space, and they have no right to engage."

"I know, Sam. They want *The Reaper* back or in bits."

I turned back towards the console; I began explaining the situation to Anne. "Okay, darling, we are sworn to protect this system. All nine planets, forty moons, and seventeen asteroid belts within this nebula," I explained. "So I need you to keep us alive."

Each side was scanning and probing for a weakness. Anne took control of the ship. The darkness outside lit up as the Navy ships opened fire, their hulls glistening.

The battle seemed to be a stalemate as Anne countered every move of the five gunships. Then came a turning point as she unleashed a massive volley of Anti-ship Missiles with ionizing warheads. It was all over in a blinding flash.

"Darling Noah, was my performance optimal?" Anne inquired.

"Anne, darling it was perfect," I replied, as I leaned back in my chair.

15 THE DISAPPEARANCE OF ROSE HARPER

I doubted Anne would surprise them the next time. Thought it best if we stayed on high alert from then on.

"Sam, make sure to keep Anne running. They would've transmitted the entire fight back to the Empyrean High Command. Soon, enough they'll be coming after us."

"Yes, Boss."

"Also, send an After Action Report to Senate Oversight," I ordered.

"Boss, you got an incoming transmission. Senate Ident Priority Ultra."

"Send it to my Ready room."

In my Ready Room, I prepared for the worst. I had a sense it was Senator Simon, but I was surprised when it turned out to be someone else.

"Madame Chairwoman! I expected a good chunk of my backside to be chewed off, but not by you."

She had given a small chuckle before she resumed a formal expression. "Thorne, I'm not calling about Sahala, you did what you had to do to survive."

"You aren't?" I asked.

"I'm calling about Rose. She's missing," the Chairwoman declared.

"Missing?"

"Yes, her last message said something about finding intelligence on one of the prisoners and its connection to Julie's death. She left before I could stop her."

I tighten my fists, and asked, "Did any of your people take a peek at this intel?"

"All we could find was the name Joe Scott

with details for the prison planet Samarian Six."

"I assume you contacted Samarian Six. What did they say?" I couldn't keep the concern out of my voice, but I didn't care at that point.

The Chairwoman's mouth twitched in amusement, but she remained solemn. "We tried. Samarian Six has gone dark."

I stood up, anxious to get started. "I'm on my way and don't worry I will move Heaven and Hell to bring her back safe."

"I don't doubt it, but if this goes wrong, I can't protect you. The Arrowhead Syndicate has been buying a lot of Senatorial support," she stated, "Good luck, Thorne."

I nodded and disconnected. I ordered Sam to change course for Samarian Six and had Anne work up an assault plan.

16 THE ASSAULT ON SAMARIAN SIX

"Boss, Samarian Six is below."

"On screen."

Samarian Six was a flawless, perfect oval white ball. The prison was an old city carved out of the surrounding ice. No one knew why there was a city was on Samarian Six in the first place. It was already abandoned when the first long haul transport discovered it centuries ago. When the Galaxy needed a prison, someone joked that they had one in Samarian Six, and the idea stuck.

Prisoners were dropped off on its surface and told which direction to walk. If they made it, they were given a warm bed, food, and a job.

The guards were mercenaries paid to live on the frozen rock for two stellar years. Afterward, they were given a warm place to live like kings for five more.

"Any signals going in or out?"

"Nothing Boss."

"Run thermal scan."

I didn't like the results. A normal scan should have show heat dots spread out as the prisoners and guards went about their work. Our scan showed two groups of heat. One large group resided on the south end of town near the armory and guardhouse. The smaller cluster of dots was on the north end near the clinic.

"We may have a riot, Sam."

"You sure, Boss?"

"Yeah, and I think the prisoners are about to be armed," I stated, "Send details to the Senate and request backup."

I didn't have time for politicians to debate or for backup to arrive. Rose was down there, and I was going after her.

"Sam, you take over the ship if anything happens to me, and coordinate the airstrike."

"Boss, I'm going with you."

I shook my head. "Sam, I need you here. Once backup gets here if you aren't here to stall, they will blow the place to smithereens with Rose and me inside."

"Yes, Boss."

"You stall for as long as Anne can receive my signal."

"Yes, Boss."

"Keep the comm signal open as long as you can."

The lander wasn't certified for cold weather climates. About halfway down to the icy surface, the cockpit window, and the rear stabilizers froze over. "Mayday! Mayday! Sam, I'm dropping like a stone," I radioed, "Towards the ground blind. All I can do is brace for impact."

The lander hit the ice, bounced and rotated again and again. I was shaken inside as if by a giant invisible hand.

I kept bouncing on the ice and skidded as a black sticky substance began to cover my left eye. Blinded, I rubbed it on the back of my hand. Red covered my wrist and fingers. It took a second for me to realize I was bleeding.

The lander stopped moving. I tried to unhook my restraint, but it was jammed. Blood was now pooling into the seat soaking into my pants, but that was the least of my worries. Panic built as I began to catch the faint whiffs of fuel. I yanked hard, slammed the release with my palm. It snapped free.

I popped the hatch, and I was hit with a freezing blast of air. The blood froze to my face. I fell out of the cockpit and ran, unsteadily in a drunken crisscrossed dizzy line away from the crash. From behind, an explosion threw me forward as my gear, guns and lander exploded.

Alone, unarmed, and wounded. Sure Anne hadn't planned the rescue this way. During the explosion, a metal shard must have hit me. My right side was sliced open, and I was holding it together as I walked.

"Sam...can you...read me?"

"Yes, Boss. Are you all right?"

Strange, but I thought I detected concern in his voice. Maybe, but I did hit my head earlier.

Pushing the thought away, I decided to ignore Sam's question, and announced,

"...not...going...make...it...immediately...after...back up...start...assault."

"Yes, Boss."

Only two people had ever escaped from this planet, and they only made it out because of blind luck and stupidity. When Simmons and Blake's time came to be dropped off, the pilot came in too low and corrected too late. They made a hard landing.

In the confusion, Simmons and Blake were rescued and transported off the world to a nearby hospital. They ended up walking out the front door without anyone noticing. I just wanted to add one more to the list--Rose.

I was sure somewhere about four, or five hundred feet east there was an internal comm link. I remembered Anne saw it earlier on the scans.

If I could make it and call the clinic, maybe Rose could hide somewhere safe. I had to just keep it together a few more feet..

17 THE VERY BAD DAY OF ROSE HARPER

"Rose, you were right," the Warden proclaimed.

He was a bully and like all bullies, he crumbled when his authority was challenged. Rose had spent three hours trying to warn him about the riot, but he just laughed in her face.

"Well that doesn't mean a whole hell of a lot right now," She answered, her face red with anger.

"Rose, I should have listened to you," the Warden continued. He was twisting his hands, nervous about the current situation.

Rose slapped his hands down, ending the constant twisting. "Snap out of it! I need everybody focused," she ordered.

He was certainly is in no shape to make decisions. She was going to have to take charge. An alarm inside the clinic began to blare with an ear shattering sound.

"Can someone shut that off, please?" She shouted over the noise, her hands up to cover her ears. People are not only pissing her off, but now the systems here had to start aggravating her too.

"That's the automated distress alarm indicating a downed craft," a technician yelled back, hands over his ears too. However, he was in no hurry to turn the noise off.

With a new sense of hope, she inquired, "Where?"

"In sector 7C-4, ma'am," he replied.

"Is there anyway to tell whether there are survivors?" Rose inquired, as she strained to understand him over the alarm. It didn't help either that her hands were still covering her ears.

"We have a comm link in the vicinity, ma'am," he answered.

"Try to patch us in and keep the lines open," she ordered before returning to the Warden.

18 THE DEATH OF NOAH THORNE

I struggled to remain conscious. My blood was draining fast. The ground behind me was a pinkish trail to where I assumed I would die.

"I'm...sorry...Rose. I tired," I proclaimed to the wind.

I could have sworn there was a comm link around here, but I couldn't find it or move another step.

"Noah, come in. Come in Noah." Rose's voice came from nowhere; it confused me. I thought I must be delirious because I heard voices.

I continued to talk to myself.

"I'm...coming...into...light. I'm...sorry...Julie, I...failed...you."

Once again, Rose's voice broke through my foggy thoughts. "Noah, this is Rose. You're near the comm link."

At the mention of the comm link, I pushed away any remaining fog. It was really Rose.

"Noah? What's going on?" Rose inquired, unable to see my relief and pain.

I said my goodbyes. "I'm...dying...bomb...this...place."

I overheard movement, and then her voice was there again. "You, Warden! Is there a way to get to him?" Rose demanded, begging a man on her end.

I began to fade, but I could still manage to overhear one last thing.

"Maintenance hatch 7A-6, and here, take this mobile regen kit," a second, manlier voice answered. It must have been a technician of sorts, but I could care less. I was dead.

19 THE RESURRECTION OF NOAH THORNE

I was dead for sixty-seven seconds. The mobile regeneration kit revived me and even fixed my wounded side. I glanced around the clinic. Everyone was frightened.

"Listen up people we are outnumbered four to one by armed prisoners and will be blasted from space anytime now," I announced to the room.

One by one, they finally snapped out of their malaise and focused.

"We need to either move to somewhere deep inside the ice and ride this out or try to make it to the old transport hub."

"Why would we go to the old hub?" a guard questioned.

"I'm hoping help will arrive before the bombs do," I answered, "My comm link to my ship is still open."

"If they drop Planet Busters we don't stand a chance of riding it out," the Warden interrupted.

"That protocol?" I asked.

"Yes."

"Okay, change of plans. We make a run for the hub," I declared.

"Sam, you get all that?" I asked over my comm link.

"I got it, Boss. Going to be tricky. I'll need to revamp some things. Make the other lander's systems ready for cold weather, not sure if it will work but I'll try."

I turned towards the group. "Let's go," I ordered.

I lead the small, fearful group out of the clinic and into the icy world of chaos. Ice and fire were everywhere, a weird contradiction.

We passed several dismembered bodies of friends, coworkers, and prisoners, as we entered the dining area.

The place was quiet. Suddenly, the prisoners sprang a trap. I threw myself in front of Rose as a large blade swung down from the ceiling. Suffered another glancing blow to the head and reopened my gash. The sound erupted all around as incoming fire came in from all directions. Six people from our group were wounded, but we continued to return fire. As the smoke cleared, at least fifteen prisoners were dead with five more severely wounded.

We continued onward to the hub, aiding our wounded. Small clashes with roving bands of prisoners revealed that tactics and training rule supreme. As the hub drew closer, we encountered the larger force and found out the real reason behind the riot.

Joe Scott was arming two of the most famous prisoners: Benito Morales and Quentin Stevens co-leaders of the Florencio Cartel.

Both had connections deep inside the Arrowhead Syndicate and the Empyrean. This was Scott's play all along the riot was just a cover for a prison break, and they were heading to the hub the same as us.

"Sam, not sure if you can overhear this, but you may see some company."

Nothing. Not good. It could have been interference, jammed by the Senate forces, or something much worse. Scott and his crew saw us. They opened fire.

We advanced and continued pushing towards the hub. The impact of the fire was heaviest near me. Most of the group was dead or wounded when we reached our destination. Rose was trying to help a guard. His left arm had just disappeared in a blast of energy, but he continued to move forward as he was shot through the other arm. Both him and Rose were brought down by a shot to his left leg. I ran back to pull her and the guard out of the line of fire. I was shot in the right leg as we crossed the threshold of the hub.

Rose was safe; the guard was dead. Resolved to hold the line until the last of those that could still walk made it to the outside landing pad, I continued to fire until my last bolt of energy.

I staggered outside, as energy exploded over my head and around my feet; and I found myself wanting one of them to end it all. The responsibility I carried on my shoulders for the dead, wounded and living was too great for one man alone.

I entered the freezing air, and my breath caught. I gazed at the empty sky and gasped in total dismay. No rescue and no hope.

I turned to face my death. The smaller angrier crowd was coming out, with Scott and Morales at the front. I didn't see Stevens anywhere. I guessed we killed him at one point.

Unarmed and wounded I fell to my knees, opened my arms, and invited my death. Head back and eyes closed, I screamed into the sky, "Death here I am! Take me now!"

Noise and explosions rocked the hub. Penetrating green balls of energy hit the prisoners, and they vanished. Loud wet sounds of sobbing and joy erupted from our group.

"You can stand up now, Boss," a nearby loudspeaker announced.

I turned. Hovering behind me was the most glorious I've sight ever seen. *The Reaper*.

After getting the wounded on board, I found Sam and asked. "How?"

"Thank Anne," he replied. "She said she had to protect her darling, so she designed a way for the entire ship to enter the atmosphere."

20 THE NIGHTMARES OF NOAH THORNE

Another endless and restless night as I lay awake staring at the ceiling, sick of wrestling with my nightmares from that day long ago. A face came into focus, pockmarked and smiling, his mouth full of black teeth.

I rushed over to my desk and entered what little details I could recall into the system. I waited and got a hit. Cam Lincoln wanted for Murder and various other crimes. Sentenced to death. Lincoln's last known location was Solas over five days ago. I can't believe we finally had a lead, and I ran to the bridge to shared the news with Sam.

"Sam, guess who I found?" I didn't wait for a response and continued, "The man who killed Julie. Set a course for Solas, and light a fire."

Solas was a desolate almost dead gray planet. If lucky, spots of red could be seen when the core expands and shifts. The main dangers were random earthquakes, hired killers, and the hurricane force winds. The intense winds continually blew across its surface.

Due to this, life on Solas happened underground. In stale recycled air bought with sweat and blood by the workers of the Fabrezie Corporation. You worked for them in the mines, or you didn't eat, sleep, or breathe in Solas. My memories of this place were unhappy ones.

Once, a group of Marshals and I were above ground. We were battered relentlessly by the winds during a five-day firefight against Fabrezie goons. We were losing and running out of options. We needed a miracle.

Leon Manning volunteered to make a run for the ship and return with air support. Three brave Marshals provided a distraction and ran out into the open laying down cover fire as Manning ran for the ship.

While they were torn apart by energy bolts and high winds he just flew away. We sat there pinned down by enemy fire and unable to stop him. The five of us left behind fought for two more days until we ran out of energy packs. I alone made it out of the mines and off Solas a stellar year later. Every intention of never returning.

"Boss, you want to search for our guy at the main factory?"

"No, Sam, I doubt our man is working. He doesn't seem the type."

"Try asking around about the local crew heads?" Sam questioned.

I shot that idea down also, and replied, "He didn't strike me as intelligent enough to run a crew, so I'm thinking low-level muscle.

Want to hire cheap unskilled muscle on Solas then Charlie's Bar is the place to go."

"Charlie's Bar?" Sam inquired.

"See that derelict building over there on the left?" I asked, pointing off in the distance. A tall building situated among a few smaller buildings, mostly homes.

"Sure, Boss."

"That is Charlie's Bar."

The building looked like it would fall at any moment. The only thing holding it up appeared to be a few mounds of dead sewer crow-rats, several broken windows, and lots of dust.

We enter the darkened bar. We're forced to step over some passed out or maybe dead patrons along the way.

"Sam, the visibility is awful in here by design. It keeps you from seeing how watered down the drinks are and how ugly the dancers and hookers are."

"Right, Boss," he replied nonplussed.

I glanced at a patron on the floor. "On the other hand, maybe its so you don't see the knife aimed at your spine. Stay vigilant," I warned.

Behind the bar was a sickly kid, a lance head, judging by his sunken eyes and green lips. Lance was the most dangerous drug to hit the systems. Idiots ingested the green poison of a Lancer worm. It kills them after sixteen uses, but they loved the high.

"Tell Charlie her markers come due," I ordered the bartender.

"I ain't telling her nothing law dog."

"You will, or I'll drop you where you stand. On the count of two. One."

The bartender dropped the glass, disappeared up the back staircase, and came down even shakier.

"I-I-I'm s-so sorry Marshal Thorne didn't know it was you. She wants you to come right up."

I slowly climbed the staircase. The door was ajar. I stood to the side of it and kicked it opened more widely with my foot. Took a deep breath and glanced inside.

Charlie was sitting at her desk a gleeful smile on her face.

"Quit goofing around. You'll give your friend the wrong first impression."

There was an expression of confusion on Sam's synthetic face.

"Sam meet Charlie; Charlie meet Sam." I gestured between them, "Charlie is my younger sister."

"Yeah, think of me as the black sheep of the family," she remarked then adds softly "How you been, big brother?"

"Okay. We got a lead on one of the men that--"

Sam took over as I began to trace the scar on my neck.

"We are here for a Cam Lincoln. He is the one who kicked the box, and ignited the assault," Sam told her.

I gazed at Charlie, eyes pleading. "I need to find him. I need names."

21 THE HUNT FOR CAM LINCOLN

Charlie came through. Her contacts found the rock Lincoln was hiding under. We approached carefully and made our way inside. As Sam and I searched, clearing each room, the worry on our faces grew.

I started to see several discarded lancer vials as we approached the last room. I didn't see any other signs of lancer use by our target back then maybe it was a new habit.

One room left. Sam scanned for booby traps, as I prepared to breach with sonic flashnades. High pitch sonic noise and disorienting flashing lights were our cover as we entered and cleared the corners. Empty. The scumbag was gone.

"Boss, over here," Sam said motioning me over.

In the middle of the room was a small burlap flour sack. The white exterior was tinged pink as it sat in a pool of dark blood. I glanced back towards the lancer vials. Sudden panic hit.

My hands trembled as they moved on their own towards the sack. The experience was like I was outside my body no longer in control. My head moved forward hands tightening on the sides of the bag. A noise. A grinding sound. Teeth grinding. My teeth. I pulled the top open and peeked inside. Charlie. No, not my sweet Charlie.

"That junkie bartender sold her out," I proclaimed aloud.

My last vestige of pride crumbled. The dam behind my eyelids broke, and I couldn't stop the flow of salty tears. I began to scream obscenities into the sky, but my voice was just wet sounds of pain and sadness. Soon, it was nothing more than, breathing and halting sighs followed by painful hiccups. I wanted to transfer my pain to someone else, and I knew who it would be. The bartender.

"Boss, you can't do this he's just a junkie it'll be murder," Sam stated.

"Take the ship and leave. Go back to Capula One and take Dogg to Rose," I ordered.

"Boss, you do this, and you're done as a Marshal."

"I'm already done."

As Sam left, I turned to the junkie passed out on the floor. I saw my sister's face; the rage flamed within me. I kicked him awake and started punching all my pain and grief into his body.

22 THE ROCK BOTTOM OF NOAH THORNE

Afterward, I climbed into every little brown bottle trying to find comfort inside. Nothing was there. I traveled from one hellhole to another begging death to pick me. I picked fights hoping someone would be better or faster on the draw.

All I got for my efforts was more bloodshed and less evil in the galaxy. I also got a reputation. I started spending more time in the saloons and jails than the hotels. I just wanted to die. I had lost everything that mattered. There was no way Rose wanted me after what I did on Solas.

After awhile I was unaware of what planet, I was on or what day it was. All I did know was it never stopped raining there, and I had to sleep in the mud. I didn't remember when I last ate solid food. I had even sunk so low that I sold my gear and badge. If I knew where it was, I would have sold the ship I stole on Solas.

"Can't be him," a thin man stated his voice filled with doubt.

"It's him," a larger man replied.

"He's so thin and weak. Should be easy," the thin man stated.

"We going to talk or kill him?" the large man challenged.

"Sure as long as I get paid when he dies," the thin man answered.

I was sure I heard voices in the alley. Maybe I could borrow some coin for a drink. I crawled from under the sidewalk my hands and feet sinking deep into the mud. I tried to stand and walk towards the voices, but my legs were sinking and making a sucking sound when I pulled them free.

"Well, we meet again," the large man proclaimed as he stepped in my way.

"Do I know you?" I asked.

"Why sure friend. I helped give you the little scar on your neck," the large man replied.

My fingers instantly flew up to my scar; eyes focused on the man. Was he one of them? If so, I hoped they would keep their guard down long enough for me to get a foot closer.

"That so. Well, could you stand me for a drink?" I asked.

"Nope. Paid to put you down not get you drunk," the thin man replied with a jeer as he leaned around the large man.

"Really? Who would do that?" I asked.

"Cam Lincoln, send his regards," the large man announced.

I wasn't in the best health or at my peak. I was sweating out months of drinking. My breathing was ragged and short. But, I launched myself at the large man.

The surprise worked I crashed into him, and we fell backward. On the ground, we struggled. He flipped me over, wrapped his huge hands around my neck, and cut off my air. My thumbs slid inside the inner corners of his eyes. As I sensed the familiar signs of unconsciousness, my thumbs found his eye sockets, and I pressed with all my might. The large man's eyes burst like two balloons, leaking black and red.

The large man screamed, and I kicked him off and rolled away. I glanced around for the other person. He was staring open-mouthed in horror at his friend. I managed to move behind him, slipped my bloody fingers into his cheeks, and pulled hard. I jerked his head as hard to the right as I could. While he was on the ground, I landed a boot heel to his nose. It must have pushed the bone into his brain because he stopped moving. I dug in the mud for his weapon.

Shoved the cold hardened steel against the large man's temple, I was finally about to have some answers.

"Now tell me the names of everyone involved that day," I ordered.

After he had told me everything, I squeezed the trigger, and walked away.

23 THE REVIVAL OF NOAH THORNE

I sold their weapons for passage off the planet. The discovery of two bodies would make the locals nervous. Sadly, I had burnt bridges all across this galaxy, and few places would welcome me back.

Only one place was left, and I had vowed never go there again. Cimarron Forty-Five. The ranch had seen better days, and I was consumed by guilt and shame that I had let her memory fall so far into rot.

I threw myself into rebuilding the place. I chopped the logs to reframe the roof and begin spudding the bark, making shakes, nailing seams, and putting on roof boards. Then, I started the weatherproofing and added two more layers. By the time, the work was done I felt rejuvenated, healthy and vigorous.

With names and a location, I could start my hunt anew. This time with no rules or laws to stop me from getting my vengeance. A long haul transport ship was leaving Cimarron Forty-Five that night, and after I had sold the ranch, I planned to be aboard as an unknown deckhand.

As I waited to board the transport ship, I took in the activity and the news coming in from the different ships. One thing was clear; I was becoming a relic of a bygone era. I could see it on the faces of the people as they passed.

On the large news screen, the Senate was promoting a new polished face to represent them as Marshal of Serpens Abyss. My former job was now more about politics than justice. If the presence of his biggest supporter, Senator Simon, were anything to go by this Marshal would be crooked and dangerous.

I was a constant reminder of the wildness some in the Senate feared. My walk, talk, and actions were evidence of dark deeds done in the name of justice, civilization, and safety by their orders. I was a vivid display of all Senator Simon despised but what made him hate me was the fact that men like me were a necessity.

He cared only about himself. I wanted to protect and serve the galaxy. I was a constant reflection of someone he could never be. An example that highlighted his personal weaknesses.

24 THE OTHER DEATH OF NOAH THORNE

"You, new guy," the first mate demanded.

"Yeah?" I replied.

"The Captain wants everyone to stop by the armory and gear up," she ordered.

"Gear up?" I asked.

"We're entering Serpens Abyss, and the Captain has a bad feeling," she continued.

"Okay. Captain's feelings always pan out?" I asked.

"Always."

I only had my gear on for more than a few seconds when the ship was rocked from the impact.

The hull breach alarms sounded on all decks. I stumbled out into the hallway it was filled with debris and fire.

"New guy secure the exposed deck and suppress these fires?" Captain ordered.

I did as ordered and sealed off the rest of the deck. Fifty people were down there.

"Any idea what hit us?" I asked after joining the Captain.

"Rammer-Jammer model. Looks new," she replied.

"Bounty hunters?" I asked.

"No, outlaws. This is a holdup," Captain explained, "Prepare to repel boarders."

They came down the hallway in armored Battlesuits firing laser blasters.

"I count ten," I announced over the noise of the explosions, crying, screaming, and gunfire.

"Got five more this side," Captain answered.

Every Battlesuit still in use was surplus gear from The Galactic War. They had one weakness. You had to hit a small light the size of an eyeball.

"Everyone aim for the red light on the left shoulder of the Battlesuit."

"What's that do?" a nearby crewmember probed.

"Watch," I said.

I tried to hit the tiny light on the twelve-foot metal Battlesuit while it fired at me, and it was more easily said than done. I had used almost an entire charge pack before I scored a hit.

The yellow energy bolt hit the red light and started a chain reaction. Within the suit, electrical circuits caused a subroutine to activate an emergency power down process. The Battlesuit ceased firing and moving. Once powered down they were no longer a threat.

"Okay, people do as the man says and aim for the red light," Captain ordered.

Most people have no idea about the buried subroutine. I was unlucky enough to field test one of the prototypes and almost died discovering the weakness.

As my confidence improved so did, my aim and I hit another. The outlaws were confused by the lack of support from the others, and chaos took over.

"We need fire support from you guys now," one outlaw shouted to the powered down suits.

"What are they doing?" another outlaw inquired.

"No idea they are just standing there," the first outlaw answered.

Someone on our side hit his red light, and we were down to five active targets in no time. The final five began to pull back to their ingress point. Moving from cover to cover, the Captain and I shut them down one by one.

One outlaw tried to eject from the Battlesuit before we shut it down. He was thrown into the ceiling, and we could hear his spine shatter. The Battlesuit fell over and collided with their ship. It broke free and spun away.

I shoved the Captain back into the other corridor as the blast doors shut sealing me inside.

The Battlesuit was sucked out and exploded. It caused a chain reaction, and the outlaw's ship exploded taking out the entire section of wall behind me. I was sucked out into space.

After ten seconds in the cold vacuum, my vision began to fade. I was close to passing out. My lungs felt as if they were about to explode. My skin was on fire with a strange bluish sunburn. As it spread along my extremities. I knew in ninety seconds I would die. Dimness continued to swallow my sight, and I began to dream. In it, I saw Julie, Rose, and Sam. Sam?

I felt my heart stop, and my lungs quit.

Felt a thump and jolt.

Bright lights.

Regen tank.

Sleep.

25 THE RESCUE OF NOAH THORNE

"You still look like crap," Rose announced as she walked through the door.

"Thanks, just what I wanted to know," I replied, as I sat up in my bed. Rose had been by every day for the past two weeks.

"Well, the most recent scan shows moderate to severe brain damage, but I'm pretty sure that was the case before you got spaced," Rose said.

"Funny. Seriously, what does it say?" I asked.

"Your fine just the same old issue with the scars it couldn't fix before," she said.

"Yeah, what's placed by hate can't ever be erased," I said as my fingers traced the scar on my neck.

I realized that I never asked something. "How did you find me?"

"We had a flag on the ranch, and when it sold, we knew it was you," Rose said.

"Why were you searching for me?" I asked, "Especially after what I did. It makes no sense."

She sat down beside me, and with some hesitancy, placed a gentle hand on my leg. "We care about you no matter what."

"Thank you," I replied, as I covered her hand with my own. "Explain how you found the transport ship."

"That was Anne. She ran the flight paths of all ships that left Cimarron Forty-Five within two days after the sell," Rose says. "She flagged any new hires crossed referenced their Ident, selected your ship."

I chuckled and squeezed her hand. "Clever girl."

"Noah, we need to talk," she said, as she changed the subject.

"Uh-oh that doesn't sound good," I replied.

"A lot of changes while you were missing. The Arrowhead Syndicate made a major play for the Senate and ousted my grandmother," she said.

I bolt upright, and stare at Rose with wide eyes, shocked. "What?"

Rose glanced away, head bowed. "Simon is now Chairman of Senate Oversight. He impounded *The Reaper* and had plans to wipe Sam and send him for defense study. He was also going to send Anne to Arrowhead for testing."

"I'm on *The Reaper* correct?" I asked as I glanced around the room.

Rose's cheeks turned red, and she began to fidget. Her hand squeezed mine.

"Yes. I didn't know what to do. You were gone. My grandmother was fighting her battles." She looked back at me but was unable to look me straight in the eyes. "So...I stole the ship and ran."

I couldn't stop smiling. It may seem like a strange reaction. But, I was so relieved it wasn't someone else. I grabbed Rose's chin; I had her meet my gaze, and said, "Rose you did the right thing never doubt that. I wouldn't be alive. Sam wouldn't be active nor would Anne."

"Thanks, Noah, I needed to hear it from someone," Rose smiled back, and she blushed even more.

26 THE TREASON OF NOAH THORNE

Insert chapter ten text here. Insert chapter ten text here. When I felt well enough, I made it to the bridge.

"Boss, incoming transmission. Senate Ident Priority Ultra."

"On screen," I said.

"You sure?" Sam inquired.

"Yeah, it concerns us all." I kept my face void of emotion with my hands clasped behind my back. I didn't want anyone to see how anxious I was.

Sam nodded and replied, "You got it, Boss."

The screen switched on and revealed the most unpleasant man in the galaxy.

"Chairman Simon, to what do we owe the pleasure," I asked.

"Cut the crap, Thorne. You 're operating a stolen Senate ship without authorization. Return to Capula One now," he ordered.

"We took a vote. You know what voting is right, Senator? The majority opinion is we are going to pass and keep the ship," I replied, "But thanks for calling and good luck in your new job."

"You listen to me you son of --"

"Screen Off," I said, "I feel that went well."

"Darling I am not sure if you are joking or serious," Anne pronounced.

"Remind me to program sarcasm in your next update," Sam uttered.

"Noah, it didn't go as well as you think."

"Why?" I asked as I turned around to find Rose looking gravely concerned.

"We all have death warrants now," Rose replied.

"They had those ready before the call if they issued them this fast," I said.

Sam walked up next to me, and asked, "So what do we do, Boss?"

"Sam, we keep going. Arrowhead's bounty hunters will still be after us. Empyrean Assassins are still going to chase us. Now, we just avoid a few overworked Marshals," I replied with a shrug. "Think of it this way. We have nothing to lose. They've taken everything from us. My family and nearly my sanity. Rose, they took your good name and your legacy. We are now free to wage war on all fronts."

27 THE LOVER OF NOAH THORNE

Rose entered my cabin, and she seemed different somehow.

"Noah, can we talk?"

"Sure, what do you need?" I asked.

Her caramel brown eyes had a raw hunger.

"You said there are no more rules, and we have nothing to lose," Rose replied as she undressed.

I took in her shapely figure. How it sat perfectly on her petite, supple frame. The seductive glow of her tanned complexion and the tight curves of her womanly body.

The shape of her pixie nose and the seductive sound of her siren voice, and desire hit me like a jolt of electric current.

She was trembling as we embraced. Her skin was elegant and smooth.

I lifted her to my lips. Her heart-shaped lips tasted like morning dewdrops and honeycomb. We kissed a long while.

I raised her into my arms moved across the room towards my bunk while whispered tantalizingly in her ear.

28 THE EVIDENCE OF JULIE REDFORD

Guilt was my feeling of choice, as I removed the last of Julie's things from my office. I realized more than ever that I needed to move on.

I was in love with Rose.

I took one last glance at our wedding day hologram; there was something odd about the size. I accessed the data and found a hidden file. Inside was a final goodbye from Julie to her father. I opened and viewed the file.

"Father, I'm getting married, and we're moving away, and that's final," she declared.

"I don't understand why you continue to throw your life away when you can do so much here for the Empyrean," Inquisitor Redford replied.

"I am trying to save lives here, and there I would be asked to develop new weapons of destruction."

"This is because of that Marshal scum isn't it?" the Inquisitor questioned, "He's there with you!"

"Noah is a good and decent man," Julie stated, pleading for her father to see things her way. He only ignored her.

"Julie, come home."

"Father you know that I can't do that so let me go."

"Fine. Tell your Marshal I will never rest until I kill him," Redford declared.

"Father, goodbye," Julie says. Her voice faded away, ending her part of the conversation.

Eerily two more voices emanate from the hologram. The link wasn't disconnected.

"Well, Inquisitor, do we have a deal?"

"Yes, you find my daughter return her to Carus, and kill Thorne. Then, she is yours."

"I will commence with recovery," the second voice pronounced, "Goodbye, Inquisitor."

"Goodbye, Secret Keeper."

29 THE VENGEANCE OF NOAH THORNE

"Sam, you can stay on board. This is personal, and there's no need for you to risk your neck."

"Boss, I'm going, and you can't stop me," Sam responded, "Besides my head is removable."

There was no point in arguing with him. "In that case, we have one primary and one secondary target. Our first objective is Secret Keeper Henry James," I say. "Perversely, he is also the head of Carus Internal Security."

"Be tough, Boss."

I brushed the remark aside, and continued, "Secondly, we eliminate the leader of the Talons.

As a personal favor for Rose and her Grandmother."

"We could dispatch her Majesty The Grand Pontiff while we're there and help the peace process along," Sam suggested.

"Why would we do that?" I asked, irritated.

"We have a unique opportunity to help millions across the galaxy," he states. "Isn't that worth a little extra effort?"

I'm embarrassed a synthetic humanoid was more human in thought and reasoning than I. This vendetta had changed and twisted my soul.

"Okay, fine," I replied, "The Grand Pontiff replaced the former Chief with her lover so they will probably be together."

"What's the plan?" Sam asked.

"James will be a handful on his own. He's the most dangerous," I said, "Forged by heat and darkness, he is the perfect Empyrean. War and conquest are as intrinsic to his DNA as height and eye color."

"So we can't go in guns blazing?" Sam asked. "How bad is this guy?"

"Right. As head of Carus Internal Security, he stands neck-deep in blood," I explained. "His first month he oversaw the torture, and execution of thirty thousand suspected 'rebels.' Boiled and roasted them alive on the holo-net as examples."

"Boss, are you trying to get me stay on the ship?"

"Nope. Just letting you know what we're in for. He's perfected the art of torture," I said. "His methods today are censorship, rumors, and public humiliation."

"That doesn't sound as bad as being boiled alive, Boss."

"If captured I'm sure he would enjoy my torture and execution," I said. "As for the Chief of the Talons, he's a trained assassin, but if we time it right, he may be distracted."

Sam begins to nod but stops. He asked, confused, "If he isn't the real Chief why are we killing him?"

"He hurt Rose a long time ago, and neither she nor her grandmother has ever forgotten."

He doesn't question any further. "Be a pleasure, Boss."

"Darling Noah, the lander is ready for departure," Anne announced.

"Thank you, Anne."

"I'm ready to go too, darling," Sam said, laughing.

"Shut up and get on board," I replied, as I shoved him in that direction. Then turned to Rose, "You have the ship."

I could tell she was unhappy. I was leaving her behind, but her grandmother had asked that she sit this mission out.

30 THE FALL OF SECRET KEEPER JAMES

James' motorcade of armed flyers and armored coach had free reign on the city streets. They didn't stop for anything, but a building falling on them may do the trick.

"You sure the timing is correct?" I asked.

"Yes, Boss."

"Mission is yours," I said.

The motorcade turned down the narrow street and crossed the bridge covering one of the many lava rivers. As the armored coach passed, the discarded box on the sidewalk Sam began his countdown.

The building started to shudder as smoke began billowing out the main floor. Lazily the building leaned and tilted to the point that gravity took over and shoved it hard into the road.

The motorcades were cut in half, and the coach was trapped under heavy stone. James stumbled out of the debris. His face and dark skin covered in a film of dust and blood. The drone landed on his neck and injected the venom.

He had three seconds; then he would pass out. In two hours, his chest would tighten, and his arms would start to tingle. In three hours, he would think his heart was stopping. His lungs would refuse to work, and he would die painfully.

It was doubtful they would find any trace of the venom during an autopsy scan since it absorbed and secreted by the body hours before death.

This nasty little concoction was a defense used by a sand worm on a distant planet now under quarantine by the Senate. The venom was harmless to the natives of the world because of an inherited immunity.

However, for off-worlders, it was a death sentence.

Sam and I rushed in and grabbed his body loaded it into the stolen ambulance and flew off. At the safe house, I woke James up and initiated the intensive interrogation.

He was tough, but the venom was already tearing apart his cells and affecting his brain chemistry. After an hour, and several broken fingers later he began to talk about that day.

31 THE SECRET OF SECRET KEEPER JAMES

Secret Keeper James had a nasty secret. He hated her Majesty and wanted power for himself. James made a deal with several within the Empyrean Legion. If they helped dispose of The Grand Pontiff, he would rule Carus in their favor.

During these clandestine meetings, James became obsessed with the Inquisitor's daughter. When she fled, James saw his chance. He proposed a deal to the Inquisitor. He would retrieve his daughter and kill the man who stole her away for approval of his marriage to her.

The deal was made, and a plan put into motion. It fell apart when we married early, sold off, and boarded a ship for Cimarron Forty-Five. James scrambled to make other arrangements, and that was his mistake.

Those that can be had quickly are not working for a reason. When we had to land on Purgatory Nine, he contacted the local outlaws. The men they provided were stupid and greedy.

"Don't lie to us," The pockmarked man said to James. "There has to be more to this than a woman."

"No. The woman is all there is. You kill the man, and bring the woman back safe," James explained.

"Plenty of women on Purgatory Nine that don't cost nowhere near this much," the pockmarked man continued.

"Just do as requested," James said.

"Still, don't make sense. All this over a woman? Has to be something more." The pockmarked man replied.

"Gold may be?" someone else asked.

"Don't be stupid just do as requested," James repeated.

But, they didn't listen. The idiots killed Julie for nothing. James' lips quivered, and tears streak down the side of his face, pooled on the table.

He had an hour of excoriating pain left to experience. That was the only thought that kept me from wrapping my fingers around his throat, and squeezing every drop of life from his worthless hide.

32 THE EXORCISM OF ROSE HARPER'S DEMON

I couldn't do it Rose needed to be the one to exorcise her demons. I told Sam to return to the ship and send her down to Carus.

"Rose, so help me if you tell your grandmother about this."

"Noah, don't worry. As long as you marry me, she can't kill you."

"So that was the plan all along?" I asked, "Have grandma tell me not to take you. Make me feel guilty until I change my mind. Then extort me into marriage."

"Well, a girl has to do something if the man she loves isn't going to ask," she replied.

"Who said I wasn't going to ask?"

"Noah, I meant ask sometime this century."

We entered the Royal bedchamber and took a few seconds to digest the opulence. Her Majesty's people had to carve homes out of molten lava, and she sat in splendor.

Gold stolen from Purgatory Nine covered almost every surface. Her nightstand could feed the entire town of Tualara. We backed into the shadows as two people bound into the room.

Intertwined they were giving each other quick little kisses, repeatedly, with the passion of a stolen moment. They seemed happy.

The man was the same brute that hurt Rose. He roughly shoved the Pontiff, onto the bed, she complained about the roughness, and he backhanded her across the face. Her nails raked at his cheek, clawing for his eyes but he just laughed.

He kissed the Pontiff again and moved to her neck. She resisted he responded by raining down a flurry of blows then yanking her head back by her hair. Rose struck with purpose and speed. Blood sprayed the bed and her Majesty.

The Pontiff tried to scream, but her voice was soundless as the poison I injected took effect. Rose tossed the bleeding body to the floor. Her Majesty passed a few seconds quickly afterward.

We returned to the ship. Sam sent a message to Free People of the Empyrean and told them the time was now for their rebellion to assume power before the Legion could react. They had an opportunity to grab the reins of their future. But, it was only the first steps of a long bloody civil war.

33 THE RECKONING OF NOAH THORNE

I still had seven outstanding debts to collect. Rose sent out feelers for a contract. We rigged it, so all seven men left on my list were hired and paid to be on Purgatory Nine.

"So what did you hire them for?" I asked.

"I didn't want them to come too heavily armed, so I told them it was a bank heist," she replied.

"Bank heist?" I asked. "Not sure that will get their attention."

"Mining payroll in the bank," she replied.

"Nice that should get them there."

"Boss, you sure you want to do this alone?"

"Yeah, the time comes when a man needs to kill his own snakes."

The men arrived late another sign of their character. The place we picked was an abandoned mining town full of derelict buildings. I got ready.

As they waited for the bank to open the next day, they enjoyed the brown bottles we left for them. I began to isolate them one by one. I started with those closest to the doors. Using a new device designed by Anne, I sent sound waves to one individual at a time.

"Did you hear that?" the chubby one, next to the door asked.

"I didn't hear anything?" someone else muttered.

"I'm going to take a look around," the chubby one announced.

"Suit yourself." The person next to him stated.

I followed the man as he exited the building used the shadows on the roof.

When he neared the top of the hotel stairs, I looped the noose over his head and pushed him off. He fell then the rope tightened with a sudden jerk. The sound of bone snapping, and he went still.

One down six to go.

"What was that?" a slender man near the door asked.

"Nothing," someone said.

"Sounded as if it came from the hotel," the slender man said, "I'm going to check."

As he walked under the balcony, I looped the rope over his head and jumped off. He flew off the ground gasping for breath. His legs kicked and twitched. I tied off the rope and moved on.

Two down five to go.

"What is it?" the man with the wandering eye inquired.

"Pete is dead. Hanged," I said.

"Hanged?"

"Yeah, come look," I said.

The man followed me outside, and I took him to his friend. He stared at his friend in confusion.

The dagger felt perfect in my hand as it whispered from its scabbard. I grabbed his hair yanked his head back as my blade tore open his throat a fountain of dark blood spraying forth.

Three down four to go. I woke up another outlaw.

"Pete's got a local girl over by the water tower," I said, "He said not to tell the others, or we'll have to share."

"Let me get my boots on." The hawkish-faced man declared with a sadistic.

"See you over there," I replied.

I'm on top of the water tower as he walked underneath.

"Pete, where are you?"

I looped the rope over his head and jumped down as he flew up. He struggled and kicked as his lungs begged for air, and he died slowly.

Four down and three to go.

I moved into the middle of the street and began to whistle a sad Novarian lullaby. The final three woke up and stumbled outside.

"I heard Morgan killed you on that mud planet," Cam Lincoln stated as he recognized me. "You ready to die like your women?"

"Draw or run, I shoot on the count of two," I said. "One."

All three drew on one. Their kind always draws on one. My hand glided to my blaster. I slid it out. When the barrel tip was just over the top, I aimed from the hip.

I tried to hit center mass at the one on the right he was the fastest. His blaster was already out and firing. He shot wide. My bolt hit his chest like a miniature yellow sun and burned its way inside.

I dove to my left and fired at Cam he was in the middle, but my aim was off, and I missed. I fired again as both gunmen's orange energy bolts plowed up the dirt around me. Cam's head disappeared in a ball of yellow, His body kept moving forward and firing wildly. After six steps, it dropped to the ground.

During all this, I rolled side to side, as orange energy bolts got closer and closer. I fired rapidly as

I stood and moved in the direction of the last man. Everything stopped.

Two of my bolts must have hit home because there was a massive hole through his chest. He dropped to his knees an expression of surprise on his face before he fell.

It took two stellar years to bring these men to justice. It cost me my sister, my freedom, and maybe even a little bit of my sanity. In the end, I gained some new friends and found love.

We vowed to become champions of all causes small and lost. *The Reaper* was now a symbol and a solution for those in need when all options had failed.

We reloaded, and prepared to unleash hell on Senator Simon and The Arrowhead Syndicate. They chose the music we will make them dance.

EPILOGUE

Six Stellar Months Later

"Rose, call Senator Simon and tell him to meet us at Janus," I ordered, "We are turning ourselves in."

"You sure about this?"

"Yes, we don't have much of a choice," I answered, "They killed your grandmother, and this needs to end."

A large gunship escort greeted us as we entered Arrowhead space. We followed their orders and flew to the main world and corporate headquarters Janus.

As we disembarked the ship, several Arrowhead mercenaries took up positions with weapons drawn, so we waited.

"This was inevitable I always win," Senator Simon said as he walked past the guards.

The CEO and CFO of Arrowhead Syndicate both drooling over their newest prize. *The Reaper* flanked him.

"The ship is better than you said Simon," the CEO said.

I knew we needed to act before more guns arrived.

"Anne now."

The area was changed into a mass of green light as Anne fired the Particle-beam weapon. It tore a rift and dematerialized all matter in its path. Simon and the others were evaporated in an instant as it flew across the platform and into the headquarters building.

Suddenly, the building began to collapse in on itself and the planet followed. We ran to the ship and tried to outrun the destruction.

The resulting compression of gasses on the core of Janus triggered a catastrophic explosion that had the force of a hundred million suns. It started to annihilate several nearby smaller planets.

They began collapsing toward the left over stellar core, and it squeezed them into a dense ball as it formed an event horizon and became a black hole. We were lucky we made it out the system, wrecked with guilt we returned to Capula One and turned ourselves in for judgment.

"Mr. Thorne, you confessed that you acted recklessly and without forethought, our investigation has uncovered that Senator Simon and the Arrowhead Syndicate were conducting illegal black hole weapons research on Janus," the Judge said. "Therefore, we were unable to tell whether the destruction was caused by your actions or if it were from an accident linked to their illegal research."

I looked at my crew and back at the Judge, confused.

"Case is dismissed, and all testimony is classified Ultra Level Nine," she says, "You are free to go. On a side note, I never like Senator Simon. Senator Harper was a dear friend, so thank you for finding her killers."

"Yes, your Honor."

"Marshal Thorne your badge is here waiting; you have a galaxy to protect and serve. You could always start with Sinity; you have unfinished work there, I believe."

The End

www.ingramcontent.com/pod-product-compliance
Lightning Source LLC
Chambersburg PA
CBHW070934130626
46555CB00001B/422